Raffle Ticket No 7
10p
Woodside Dry Cleaners. receipt for Jacket and bow tie.
Mouse
STAMFORD, LINCS.
Dear Mouse
Weather fine and sunny. Have been Picnicing on common. Love Rat.
Mr. Mouse
The woods
(Just past Rabbits hole)

your sight
test is on
2.30pm
Mole
you are cordially
invited to Rabbits
birthday party.
Bring a cake. R.S.V.P.
SCUNTHORPE
-ON-SEA.
Having a
lovely time,
wish you
were here!
from Rabbit.
To Mole esq.
The Woods
(near owls
tree)
(Don't know Postcode)
Mole
To be kept
SEAT No
7.30
off you

For Alison de Vere, with thanks
~ J. D and J. M ~

向埃利森·德维尔致谢
—— 乔伊斯·邓巴和詹姆斯·梅休

中英双语

老鼠和鼹鼠

真是幸福啊

[英]乔伊斯·邓巴 著　[英]詹姆斯·梅修 绘　仇春卉 译

中信出版集团 | 北京

图书在版编目（CIP）数据

老鼠和鼹鼠. 真是幸福啊 / (英) 乔伊斯·邓巴著；(英) 詹姆斯·梅修绘；仇春卉译. -- 北京：中信出版社, 2021.10（2025. 4重印）
ISBN 978-7-5217-3411-9

Ⅰ. ①老… Ⅱ. ①乔… ②詹… ③仇… Ⅲ. ①儿童故事-图画故事-英国-现代 Ⅳ. ①I561.85

中国版本图书馆CIP数据核字(2021)第151261号

老鼠和鼹鼠·真是幸福啊

著　　者：［英］乔伊斯·邓巴
绘　　者：［英］詹姆斯·梅修
译　　者：仇春卉
出版发行：中信出版集团股份有限公司
（北京市朝阳区东三环北路27号嘉铭中心　邮编　100020）
承 印 者：北京启航东方印刷有限公司

开　　本：889mm × 1194mm　1/16　　印　　张：3.25　　字　　数：60千字
版　　次：2021年10月第1版　　印　　次：2025年4月第9次印刷
京权图字：01-2021-1891
书　　号：ISBN 978-7-5217-3411-9
定　　价：28.00元

出　　品：中信儿童书店
图书策划：如果童书
策划编辑：安虹　　责任编辑：孙婧媛　安虹　　营销编辑：张远　邝青青　张超
封面设计：谢佳静　　内文排版：王莹

目录

吊床

老鼠找到一张很大的网。他把网的一头绑在树枝上，另一头绑在篱笆桩上。

“这样就能挂成一张很棒的吊床了。”老鼠自言自语道。

鼹鼠来看看老鼠在干什么。

“这张吊床挂得不错嘛！”鼹鼠说。

“我也觉得。”老鼠说，“我现在就要舒舒服服地躺到上面，透过绿叶看着蓝天，听着鸟儿歌唱。”

“还让轻风把你摇来摇去。”鼹鼠说。

“对的。”老鼠说。

老鼠正打算爬上去，鼹鼠突然说：“老鼠，等等！”

“怎么了？”老鼠问。

“我觉得这东西不安全呀。”

“为什么不安全呢？”老鼠问。

“你不知道躺上去之后会发生什么意外呀。比如说，树枝可能会折断，砸到你头上。”

“不会的。”老鼠说着，开始往吊床里爬。

“可是老鼠啊，”鼹鼠说，“也许小鸟的歌声太响亮，把你吵得直头痛。”

“我喜欢小鸟的歌声。”老鼠说着，又继续往吊床里爬。

“也许风吹得太厉害，你摇摇晃晃的会头晕。”鼹鼠说。

“轻风会吹得刚刚好，把我摇得舒舒服服。”老鼠说着，还要往吊床里爬。

“不行，老鼠，我不能让你冒险！我要亲自帮你试一下，确保这张吊床很安全！”说完，鼹鼠将老鼠一把推开，自己爬进了吊床里。

“啊！”鼹鼠长长地叹了一口气，伸了伸懒腰，闭上了眼睛。

“感觉怎么样，鼹鼠？”老鼠问。

“很不舒服！”鼹鼠说，“要想让这张吊床舒服点儿，就得加一两个靠垫才行。老鼠，你能去拿些靠垫过来吗？”

于是，老鼠去拿了两个靠垫回来，递给鼹鼠。

“现在感觉怎么样，鼹鼠？”老鼠问。

“还是不舒服。”鼹鼠说，“也许来一罐饼干就能好点儿了。老鼠，你能去拿些饼干过来吗？”

于是，老鼠去拿了一罐饼干给鼹鼠。

“现在怎么样，鼹鼠？”老鼠问。

“嗯……”鼹鼠拿起一块饼干，大声咀嚼起来，“风不太大，鸟儿没有叫得太响，树枝也没有砸下来。可如果想追求完美的话，这饼干就得配上鲜榨柠檬茶。老鼠，你能去做点儿柠檬茶吗？”

于是，老鼠去做了一些鲜榨柠檬茶。

“好啦，鼹鼠！”老鼠说，“两个靠垫，一罐饼干，又来一点儿鲜榨柠檬茶。现在你可以确定这个吊床真的又安全又舒服了。谢谢你，鼹鼠。”

“哦，其实还不能完全确定呢。”鼹鼠说道，抿了一小口柠檬茶，“为了百分之百确定，我还需要再试好大一会儿，而且不能有旁人打扰。就请你再给我递些饼干和柠檬茶，让我独自待一会儿吧。”

于是，老鼠又给了他一些饼干和柠檬茶。鼹鼠接过来，舒舒服服地躺好。“幸福极了！”他感叹道，“真是幸福啊！”

话音刚落，吊床就塌了。

鼹鼠一下子摔在地上，饼干和柠檬茶洒得到处都是。鼹鼠吓呆了，一句话也说不出来。

“天哪，鼹鼠！”老鼠说，“你说得对，原来吊床真的不是那么安全。多亏了你，我才没有摔痛屁股！你真是我的好朋友！不过这次，我一定会把吊床拴得牢牢的。现在就请你在靠垫上歇一下，也不用给我递饼干和柠檬茶，因为我只要有吊床就很幸福了。”

就这样，老鼠幸福地躺到了吊床上。

眼镜

“我的眼镜丢了。”鼹鼠说。

“哪副眼镜？”老鼠问。

“我专门戴着用来找其他眼镜的那副丢了。”鼹鼠说。

老鼠掀开鼹鼠的扶手沙发坐垫，在两侧仔细翻了翻，摸到一副被压弯的眼镜。“是这一副吗？”他问。

鼹鼠戴上眼镜盯着老鼠看，眼前有点儿模糊。

“不是。”鼹鼠回答，顺手把眼镜推到脑袋上，“不是这一副。”

老鼠趴在地上，爪子伸进橱柜底下摸索，又掏出一副眼镜来。“是这副吗？”他问。

鼹鼠戴上后四处看了一圈，眼前有点儿蒙眬。

“不。”鼹鼠说着，把它往上推到上一副眼镜前面，“这副也不是。”

老鼠走进卧室，拿起床单被子用力抖了抖，一副眼镜掉了下来。“这副呢？”他问。

鼹鼠戴上眼镜，跌跌撞撞地走进过道里，鼻子一下子撞在栏杆上，结果鼻子上的这副又与脑袋上的其他眼镜挤到了一起。

“不。”鼹鼠说，“绝对不是这一副。”

老鼠认真地翻找着放袜子的抽屉，又沿着挂茶杯的排钩一个一个地查看，还在壁橱里仔细搜寻。他找到的眼镜越来越多，鼹鼠把它们一一戴上，可是每个都不合心意。最后，他脑袋上堆满了一长串亮闪闪的眼镜。

老鼠受够了。“鼹鼠！”他说，“你为什么需要那么多副眼镜呢？”

“为什么？”鼹鼠手里拿着一副眼镜转个不停，“为什么？”

“对啊，为什么呢？”

“因为我不仅要戴一副，还需要其他的备用啊。

我需要一副专门在黑暗里戴的眼镜，

还需要一副专门在亮光里戴的眼镜。

我需要一副专门用来看红色东西的眼镜，

还需要一副专门用来看绿色东西的眼镜。

我需要一副专门用来看小件东西的眼镜，

还需要一副专门用来看大件东西的眼镜。

我需要一副专门用来看近处东西的眼镜，还需要一副专门用来看远处东西的眼镜。

我需要一副眼镜专门看我想记住的东西，

还需要一副眼镜专门看我想忘记的东西。

我需要一副眼镜专门看真实的东西，

还需要一副眼镜专门看我想象出来的东西。

我需要一副眼镜专门看让我难过的东西，

还需要一副眼镜专门看让我开心的东西。

我需要一副眼镜专门看我的好朋友老鼠，

也需要一副眼镜专门寻找那些丢了的眼镜，

还需要……”

“你还需要好朋友老鼠帮你找到那些眼镜！”老鼠从脏衣篮里探出头来，打断了鼹鼠的话，“肯定是这副了吧！”他补充道，“因为所有地方我都已经找遍了。”

鼹鼠戴上这副眼镜，很开心地环顾四周。

“找到啦！就是这副！”他大声说，“专门用来寻找其他眼镜的眼镜！”

鼹鼠开始四处找。

他把放袜子的抽屉翻了个遍。

他沿着挂茶杯的排钩一个一个地查看。

他在壁橱里仔细搜寻。

可是一副眼镜也找不到。

“老鼠啊，这回麻烦大了！”他说，“我还是找不到其他眼镜呀！”

“鼹鼠。”老鼠说。

“什么事？”鼹鼠说。

“你照镜子的时候，戴哪副眼镜？”

“当然是最好的那副了——就是用玳瑁做镜框的那副。”

“是这副吗？”老鼠把玳瑁眼镜移到那串眼镜的最前面，然后带着鼹鼠走到镜子前。

鼹鼠看到了自己脑袋上的一长串眼镜。“哎呀，老鼠！”他说，“要是我有这么多双眼睛，就能够把所有东西一眼看清了。”

接落叶

这是一个秋天的早晨，外面雾蒙蒙的，叶子开始从树上飘下来。

“老鼠，你看。”鼹鼠说，“树叶已经开始落了。”

“有个说法你听过吗？”老鼠说，“据说如果你能接住一片落叶，就会一直走运到年底。”

“我们试试呗。”鼹鼠说。

“我们去树林里试吧。”老鼠说，“那里全是树木和叶子，成功的机会会大得多。”

很快，他们来到了树林里。

一阵风吹过，树上的叶子纷纷飘落。

老鼠和鼹鼠伸出爪子四处跑，想接住一片叶子。

"没接住！"老鼠说。

"没接住！"鼹鼠说。

"又没接住！"老鼠说。

"我也是！"鼹鼠说。

叶子不停地飘呀飘，老鼠和鼹鼠不停地跑呀跑，却连一片落叶也没接住。

他们坐到了树桩上，想歇一歇。

“这事儿看起来容易，做起来难呀。”老鼠说。

“我们要用科学的方法解决这个问题。”鼹鼠说，“你想想，叶子不是直直地落下来的，而是转来转去、打着旋儿。如果我们也跟着转来转去、盘旋翻滚，说不定就能接住一片了。”

正说着，鼹鼠看见了一片落叶。

“你看着，”鼹鼠说，“我给你示范一下。”

叶子在空中飘舞，鼹鼠就在叶子下面跟着翩翩起舞。

叶子转来转去，鼹鼠也转来转去。

叶子打着旋儿，鼹鼠也盘旋翻滚。

老鼠坐在旁边，一动不动地看着。

“中！”鼹鼠说着，踮起脚尖转了最后一个圈。眼看着落叶快要落入爪子里，鼹鼠突然被一根树枝绊了一下……

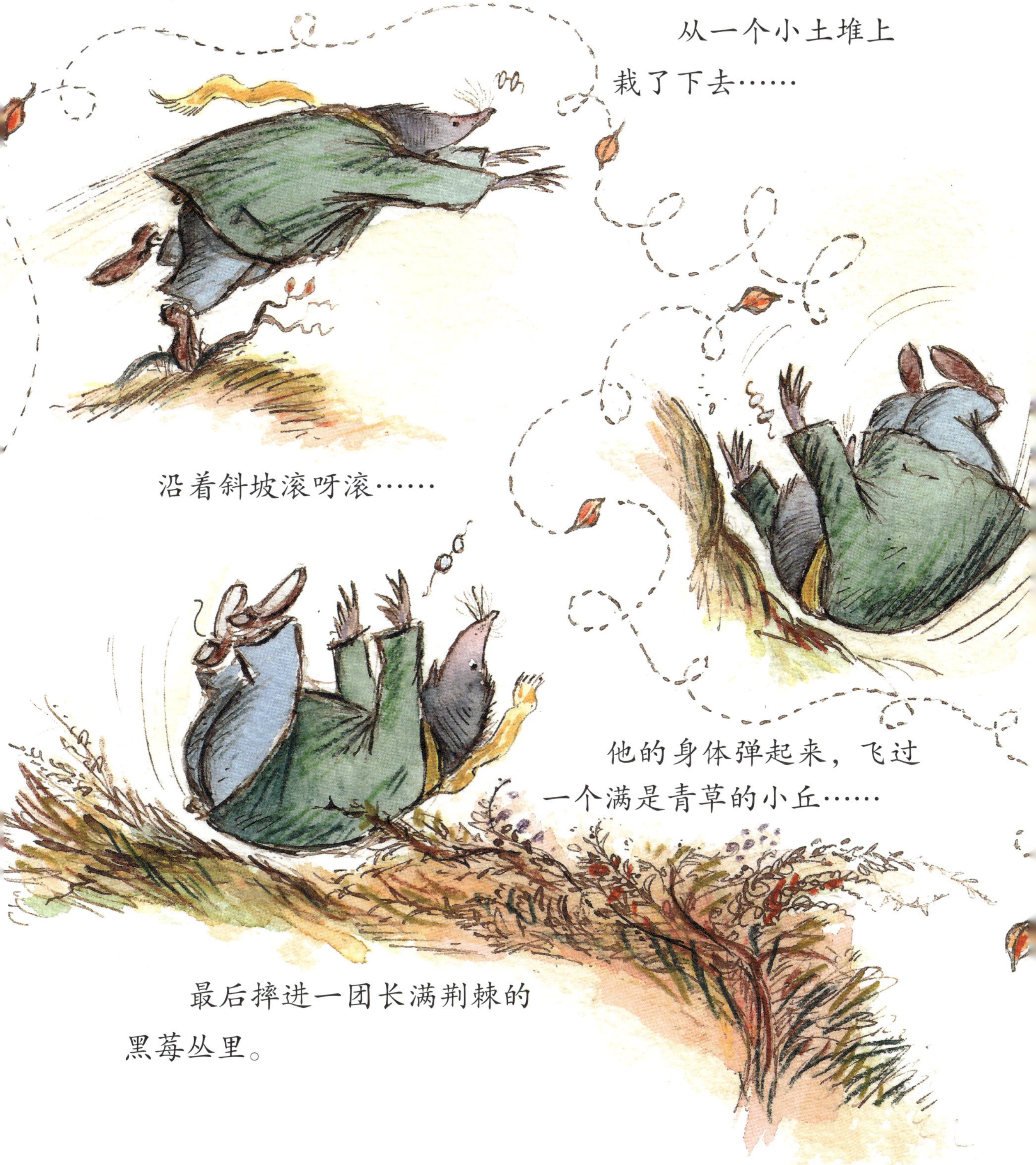

从一个小土堆上栽了下去……

沿着斜坡滚呀滚……

他的身体弹起来，飞过一个满是青草的小丘……

最后摔进一团长满荆棘的黑莓丛里。

鼹鼠想接住的那片落叶，却直接落在了老鼠的膝盖上。

“鼹鼠，你没事吧？”老鼠喊道。

老鼠只看见鼹鼠的大鼻子。突然，一只爪子从黑莓丛里伸出来，爪子里还攥着一片褐色的树叶。“老鼠快看！”鼹鼠喊道，“看看我爪子里有什么！虽然这不是我想接住的那片，不过怎么说也是一片落叶呀！”

“我觉得只要是落叶就行了，随便哪片都一样。”老鼠说着，把自己那片叶子扔到地上，“来，我把你从黑莓丛里拉出来。”

“你怎么样，老鼠，你最后接到落叶了吗？”

“没有，鼹鼠，我没接到。我不像你会跳落叶舞呀。”

“哎哟！”鼹鼠呻吟着说，“我浑身上下都擦破了，还扎了好多刺！”

“没关系的。”老鼠说，“你已经证明了你是一只具有科学精神的鼹鼠。”

“这倒是。”鼹鼠说。

“而且你会一直走运到年底。”老鼠补充道。

“没错！”鼹鼠说，“等明年吧，等明年我帮你也接一片落叶！”

Happy Days for MOUSE & MOLE

Joyce Dunbar and James Mayhew

The Hammock

Mouse found a large piece of net. He tied one end to the branch of a tree and the other end to a fence post.

'This will make a very good hammock,' said Mouse to himself.

Mole came to see what he was doing.

'That makes a very good hammock,' Mole said.

'That's what I thought,' said Mouse. 'Now I am going to lie on my hammock and look at the sky through the leaves and listen to the singing of the birds.'

'And let the breeze rock you gently to and fro,' said Mole.

'That's right,' said Mouse.

He was about to get into the hammock when Mole said, 'Wait a minute, Mouse!'

'What for?' asked Mouse.

'It doesn't look safe to me.'

'Why not?' asked Mouse.

'You never know what might happen. A branch might break off the tree and fall on your head.'

'I don't think so,' said Mouse, starting to climb into

his hammock.

'But Mouse,' said Mole, 'the birds might sing too loudly and give you a headache.'

'I like birdsong,' said Mouse, trying once more to get into the hammock.

'The breeze might rock you too much and make you feel dizzy,' said Mole.

'The breeze will rock me just right,' said Mouse, still trying to get into his hammock.

'No, Mouse, I can't let you do it. I, Mole, will test it for you. I'll make sure it really is safe.' And, pushing Mouse out of the way, Mole clambered into the hammock.

'Aaah!' sighed Mole, stretching out and closing his eyes.

'How does it feel, Mole?' asked Mouse.

'Terrible,' said Mole. 'What you need to make this hammock comfortable is a cushion or two. Will you go and fetch them, Mouse?'

So Mouse went and got two cushions. He gave them to Mole.

'How does it feel now, Mole?' asked Mouse.

'Awful,' said Mole. 'Perhaps a jar of biscuits would make it all right. Will you bring a jar of biscuits, Mouse?'

So Mouse fetched a jar of biscuits for Mole.

'How is that now, Mole?' asked Mouse.

'Hmmm,' said Mole, munching one of the biscuits. 'The breeze isn't too strong. The birds are not singing too loudly. The branches are not falling from the tree. But to make it really perfect, you need some fresh lemonade to go with the biscuits. Would you go and make some, Mouse?'

So Mouse made some fresh lemonade.

'There you are, Mole!' he said. 'Two cushions. A jar of biscuits. Some fresh lemonade. Now you have made sure the hammock is really safe and comfortable. Thank you, Mole.'

'Oh, I am not really sure,' said Mole, sipping the lemonade. 'To make really sure, I need to test it for a good long time. I need to be left all alone. Now, you just pass me more biscuits and lemonade and leave me for a while.'

Mouse passed more biscuits and lemonade. Mole settled himself down. 'Bliss!' he sighed. 'Such bliss!'

But no sooner had he said these words than the hammock broke.

Mole went crashing to the ground and the biscuits

and lemonade went flying. Mole was too astonished to speak.

'Why, Mole!' said Mouse. 'You were right. The hammock wasn't safe after all. You saved me a nasty bump. What a good friend you are! But I'll fix it properly this time. Now, you just rest on the cushions. And don't bother about lemonade and biscuits for me. I'll be happy with just the hammock.'

And Mouse was.

Spectacles

'I've lost my glasses,' said Mole.

'Which pair?' asked Mouse.

'The pair I need to find my other pairs of glasses,' said Mole.

Mouse lifted the cushion from Mole's armchair and groped around down the sides. He fished out a bent pair of spectacles. 'This pair?' he asked.

Mole tried them on. He peered dimly at Mouse.

'No,' said Mole, pushing the glasses up onto his head. 'Not this pair.'

Mouse got down on all fours and felt under the kitchen dresser. He pulled out another pair of spectacles. 'This pair?' he asked.

Mole put them on. He blinked blearily around the room.

'No,' said Mole, pushing the glasses up in front of the others. 'Not this pair either.'

Mouse went into the bedroom and gave the bedclothes a good shake. Out fell another pair of spectacles. 'This pair?' he asked.

Mole put them on and stumbled out into the hall. He bumped his snout against the bannister so that the glasses got pushed up with the others.

'No,' said Mole. 'Definitely not this pair.'

Mouse searched in the sock drawer. He looked along the cup hooks. He rummaged in the store cupboard. He brought out more and more glasses. Mole tried them on, one after the other, until the top of his head was crowned with a row of shining spectacles.

Mouse was feeling fed up. 'Mole,' he said. 'Why do you need so many pairs of glasses?'

'Why?' said Mole, twirling a pair of spectacles. 'Why?'

'Yes, why?'

'Well, I need glasses to wear, and glasses to spare.

I need glasses for the dark, and glasses for the light...

I need glasses for things that are red, and glasses for things that are green...

I need glasses for things that are small, and glasses for things that are large...

I need glasses for things that are near, and glasses for things that are far...

I need glasses for things that I want to remember, and glasses for things I want to forget...

I need glasses for things that are real, and glasses for things I imagine...

I need glasses for things that make me sad, and glasses for things that make me happy...

I need glasses to see my dear friend Mouse, and I need glasses to find lost glasses, and...'

'And a dear friend Mouse to find those glasses!' interrupted Mouse from the laundry basket. 'And it must be this pair,' he added, 'for there is nowhere else to look.'

Mole put them on. He stared happily around the

room.

'Yes, this is the pair,' he exclaimed. 'My glasses for finding other glasses!'

He began to search around.

He scrabbled through the sock drawer.

He looked along the cup hooks.

He hunted in the store cupboard. But he didn't find a single pair of spectacles.

'Mouse, this is serious,' he said. 'I still can't find my other glasses.'

'Mole,' said Mouse.

'What is it?' said Mole.

'Which pair do you use to look at yourself?'

'My best pair, of course, with tortoiseshell frames.'

'This pair?' said Mouse, moving them to the front of the row and leading Mole to the mirror.

Mole saw the row of glasses on his head. 'Why, Mouse!' he said. 'If only I had as many pairs of eyes, I'd be able to see everything at once!'

Catch a Falling Leaf

It was a misty autumn morning. The leaves were beginning to fall.

'Look, Mouse,' said Mole. 'The leaves are falling already.'

'You know what they say,' said Mouse. 'If you can catch a falling leaf, you will be lucky for the rest of the year.'

'Let's try,' said Mole.

'We will have a better chance in the wood,' said Mouse. 'It is full of leaves and trees.'

They were soon on their way through the wood. A breeze through the trees sent down some leaves in a flurry.

Mouse and Mole tried to catch one, running around with outstretched paws.

'Missed!' said Mouse.

'Missed!' said Mole.

'Missed again!' said Mouse.

'So did I,' said Mole.

The leaves kept falling and falling. Mouse and Mole

kept trying and trying. Every time they missed.

They sat down on a tree stump for a rest.

'It's not as easy as it looks,' said Mouse.

'We need to be scientific,' said Mole. 'You see, the leaves are not falling straight down. They spin this way and that, they whirl and they twirl. Perhaps if we also spin this way and that, whirl and twirl, we will be able to catch a falling leaf.'

That moment, Mole spied a single falling leaf.

'Just watch,' said Mole. 'And I'll show you.'

The leaf danced round through the air. Mole danced down on the ground.

The leaf spun this way and that. Mole spun that way and this.

The leaf whirled and twirled.

Mole twirled and whirled, while Mouse sat still and looked on.

'Here it comes,' said Mole, doing a final pirouette. But just as the leaf seemed about to fall into his paw, Mole tripped over a branch... stumbled over a hillock... rolled down a bank... bounced over a grassy hummock... until he landed in a prickly bramble bush.

The leaf Mole was trying to catch landed straight in

Mouse's lap.

'Are you all right, Mole?' called Mouse.

Only Mole's snout could be seen, and a paw that clutched a brown leaf. 'Look, Mouse!' he yelled. 'See what I have in my paw. It wasn't the one I was chasing, but it's a falling leaf just the same.'

'I'm sure one leaf is as good as another,' said Mouse, dropping his own leaf to the floor. 'Here, let me help you out of that bush.'

'What about you, Mouse? Did you manage to catch a leaf?'

'No, Mole, I didn't. I can't do a leaf dance like yours.'

'Oooh,' moaned Mole. 'I am scratched and stung all over.'

'Never mind,' said Mouse. 'You have proved you are a scientific mole.'

'I have,' said Mole.

'And you will be lucky for the rest of the year,' added Mouse.

'I will,' said Mole. 'And next year, I shall catch a leaf for you.'

Raffle Ticket No7
10p
Woodside Dry Cleaners. receipt for Jacket and bow tie.
Mouse
STAMFORD, LINCS.
Dear Mouse,
Weather fine and sunny. Have been Picnicing on common. Love Rat.
Mr. Mouse
The woods
(Just past Rabbits hole)

Mole
SCUNTHORPE-ON-SEA
Having a lovely time wish you were here! from Rabbit
To Mole esq. The Woods (Near Owls tree) (Don't know Postcode)
Mole
you are cordially invited to Rabbits birthday party. Bring a cake. R.S.V.P.
OPTICIAN
your sight test is on
to be kept